When The Elephant Visits Her Grammy

When the Little Elephant visits her Grammy, they bake cookies.

When the Little Elephant visits her Grammy, they build a fort.

When the Little Elephant visits her Grammy, they go for a walk.

When the Little Elephant visits her Grammy, they draw with sidewalk chalk.

When the Little Elephant visits her Grammy, they play at the park.

When the Little Elephant visits her Grammy, they make crafts.

When the Little Elephant visits her Grammy, they put puzzles together.

When the Little Elephant visits her Grammy, they look at family photos.

When the Little Elephant visits her Grammy, they read a book together.

When the Little Elephant visits her Grammy, they plant flowers.

When the Little Elephant visits her Grammy, they bird watch.

When the Little Elephant visits her Grammy, they go on a picnic.

When the Little Elephant visits her Grammy, she gets lots of hugs.

Made in United States
Orlando, FL
20 December 2024

56301043R00015